THE PETS' REVOLT!

(Hardcover title: <u>Mat Pit and the Tunnel Tenants</u>)

Written and illustrated by

SHEILA GREENWALD

Cover illustration by Joel Naperstek

SCHOLASTIC INC.
New York Toronto London Auckland Sydney Tokyo

FOR GEORGE

ISBN 0-590-62014-2

12 11 10 9 8 7 6 5 4 3 2 1   10   3 4 5 6 7/8

Printed in the U.S.A.   11

THE PETS' REVOLT!

ONE

ON the sixteenth floor of the South East Wing of the Princess Gardens Terrace Apartment House, in an apartment with a C on its door, lived a boy named Mathew Pit. Mathew (or Mat as he was most often called) had problems which were almost too great for a nine-year-old boy to bear.

For one thing he had just lost his gerbil, which he regarded as the creature most dear to him. He had opened the cage to clean it out, holding the gerbil for a moment in the crook of his arm where it seemed very still and content. Suddenly it leaped like a flying squirrel and scampered across the floor and behind the radiator. Where the gerbil went was the gerbil's own secret.

Not knowing how to think like a gerbil or anyone but Mathew Pit, Mat had no idea where to look. Mat didn't cry—he prided himself on not crying—but he knew that he'd lost the creature who was closer to him than any other.

For another thing, Mat's mother and father expected much of him. Good report cards for one and being good at games for another and lots of friends for the last. Mat Pit had none of these things. He had a gerbil (at least until it ran under the radiator). The gerbil, whose name was Sparky, never expected Mat to be anything but what he was. As long as he was fed sunflower seeds and lettuce leaves and tops of carrots everything was fine between Mat and Sparky.

The night the gerbil disappeared, Mat told his parents at dinner.

"Does that mean that little rodent is wandering around loose in this house?" cried Mrs. Pit nearly dropping the beans.

"Perhaps now Mat will devote more time to his studies, and not be forever mooning over that furry beast," said Mr. Pit, winking good-naturedly at Mat. Mat smiled back at his father because his father's winks were very nice and very rare.

After dinner Mat was sent to his room to finish his homework. It seemed he had more homework than there was water in the Hudson River. He knew he had to do it well because the school had told his parents that he was always dreaming and not paying attention. Mat's parents were upset about that. They wanted him to work as hard as he could. They both did their work well, they said, and they expected the same of Mat. Mrs. Pit worked

hard as a teacher and Mr. Pit worked hard in his shop. They told Mat they never got things done by dreaming and neither would he.

As Mat sat at his desk trying to work, he had the feeling that someone was staring at him. He looked around his room. Everything was the same, except for Sparky's empty cage. Nobody was there and yet the feeling that a pair of eyes was watching him didn't go away. Finally he had to get up and check some places that were not easy to see from his desk. He looked under his bed, he looked in his closet, and he looked under the radiator. Except for a couple of dust balls, the stub of a pencil, and a broken plastic spoon, there seemed to be nothing there. Then Mat realized there was something. It was a hole in the wall, a small vent hole with the rim of a pipe coming out of it, just the sort of hole Sparky would like to get into.

Mat peered down the hole into a still

darker space. As he stared into the darkness he realized that if Sparky was down there, he would be without food. Before he returned to his desk, he placed a pile of sunflower seeds underneath the vent hole. He wondered if they would be eaten.

TWO

THE following morning, as soon as he woke up, Mat was on his knees in front of the radiator. The sunflower seeds were gone. There wasn't one husk left. He put more seeds out and added some leaves from the tops of celery and a few carrots.

The hours at school passed more slowly than usual that day. Mat couldn't wait till he got home to see if the food was gone.

It was completely gone, not a scrap left. Mat smiled into the hole. "Hey, Sparky. You sure are hungry. I bet you're thirsty, too. I better get you something to drink." Mat placed a small dish of water just beside the hole. "Take care of yourself, Sparky," he said. "And if you feel like it please come and see me. I really miss you."

Mat sat and gazed into the hole for quite some time, but no Sparky appeared and so he decided that Sparky was not ready to come out. Mat thought Sparky must be enjoying his freedom and having an adventure and didn't want to get the food till Mat was gone.

Later that night, as he sat working over his math book, Mat again felt that a pair of eyes was watching him, but when he looked under the radiator, no creature was there.

In the morning, the water dish was empty. All the food was gone. Mat filled the dish and left fresh food before he went to school. Again he could think of nothing but getting home to see what had happened. Several times his teacher asked him what he was dreaming about and to please pay attention.

When Mat got home he found the food and water were gone. "Hey, Sparky, can't I just see you for a minute?" he said softly into the hole. "I won't try to catch you, I promise. I just want to see if you're okay." Mat waited, but the hole was as dark and still as ever. Finally he went to fill the water dish. He tried not to look at Sparky's empty cage which he hadn't the heart to put away. He placed seeds and salad beside the hole and sat down to his homework.

Again he felt that eyes were staring at him. Finally his back hairs bristled and his neck grew hot under the stare. He could not sit for another minute without checking the vent hole. It took his eyes a second to get accustomed to the darkness under the radiator, but when they did, he saw looking straight back at him from the dark circle of the hole a pair of deep bright eyes.

The expression of the eyes was intense, but friendly. The eyes belonged to a small gray mouse.

"Where did you come from?" said Mat, who was disappointed not to find Sparky.

"Originally from the Ninety-fourth Street Pet Shop. Thence to apartment 17A in the Princess Gardens Terrace East Wing. I resided for a time with a family named Klugman, mainly as the responsibility of a child named Fred. Fred gave yours truly a hard time. Dropped me twice, forgot to change the water and leaned too heavily on sandy lettuce for the menu."

"Where do you live now?" said Mat.

"In there." The mouse pointed to the vent hole.

"Have you seen Sparky in there?" said Mat.

"Certainly I have, and I bring a message from him as well as all the rest of us."

"The rest of you?" Mat was astonished.

"The community. . . . We have twenty-seven gerbils, thirty-nine hamsters, sixty mice, five guinea pigs, and there's a dear old rabbit in 14C who's longing to join us, but can't quite squeeze in. We've had several babies so our population is certainly expanding, but the way that tunnel dips and slides and rises and bends, there's room and privacy enough for everyone."

The mouse preened his whiskers and looked at the floor, pausing dramatically. "And now for my message." He cleared his throat and extended his paw. "My name is Jester. We have been watching you. We need a friend whom we can trust. We think we can trust you." Jester said this slowly and with great seriousness. "We also thank you for the food and water which you have given with no traps attached. You see, our experience with peo-

ple has taught us that they are tricky.
Sparky tells us you are different. He says
you are very lonely. Your parents and
your school make you unhappy. We rodents are not so hard on our children. Of
course we may eat them from time to time,

but that is our nature."

The mouse sniffed and cocked his head to one side. "I must be off now, they're calling me. Do keep up the food supply. We usually have to forage in people's apartments after dark and often the work is hazardous."

Jester put out his paw to be shaken again. "Adieu then, dear Mat," he said. "You are a friend to us and we are faithful to our friends." With these words he hopped into the hole and was gone.

Later that night, as Mat lay wide awake in his bed, he was suddenly filled with joy. He knew something that his parents didn't know. He knew something that nobody else in the world knew. Where it would lead to or what it meant he didn't know, but he was certain that things were going to be different for him. Mat couldn't have dreamed just how different his life would be from the day of his strange discovery.

THREE

FOR one month Mat saw no creature from the community. He knew they were alive and well because the food and water he left for them continued to disappear very quickly. It gave him pleasure to put out the full dishes and find them empty. He felt he was helping the whole community to survive.

Then one Friday morning just one month after his conversation with Jester, Mat woke up to a day he would never forget. First of all he couldn't seem to wake up, but had to be hauled out of bed by his father. His shirt went on backwards and had to be pulled off and turned around and his shoes were on the wrong feet and had to be changed. He spilled his milk causing his mother a headache and after that there was nothing to do but set off for school.

As Mat waited for the self-service elevator to open he was suddenly very happy. He remembered Jester and he realized that just as the big elevator was rising and lowering in its shaft filled with human tenants, there were those smaller tunnels in which fragile furry creatures were beginning to scurry into the business of their day. This thought so cheered Mat Pit that when he arrived in the lobby of his building a great smile crossed his face.

"What are you smiling for?" said Edward Harbock.

"I don't know," Mat said quickly.

"Boy, are you dumb," said Edward.

"Don't be unkind," said Edward's mother.

It was Mat's misfortune to have to

walk to school every morning with Edward and his mother. Mrs. Harbock only walked part of the way with them leaving them at the subway which she took to work.

"Well, he doesn't even know what he's smiling for," Edward said. "How dumb can you get?"

"He probably knows but doesn't want to tell you, isn't that so, Mat?" said Mrs. Harbock. Mrs. Harbock was always putting words into everybody's mouth and thoughts into their heads. She was like a wizard. Mat could only lower his eyes and pray she couldn't read right through them into the center of his brain.

Edward pushed open the door of the Princess Gardens and they stepped into a sooty spring morning. No sooner had they taken three steps than Edward began to wheeze and gasp.

"Oh, boy, the pollution level," he whispered.

"It's his allergy," said Mrs. Harbock to the superintendent. She gave Edward a pill which he swallowed without water. He seemed to recover after a few minutes and by the time they reached the corner he could talk again.

"How far did you get in the new math book?" he said to Mat.

Mat decided not to answer the question.

"I said, how far did you get in the math?" Edward repeated.

"I've done it all," said Mat smiling up at the gray sky.

"You did not," said Edward. "You can't add one and one."

"Done it all," Mat said, still smiling. "I used my magic."

"What magic?" said Edward.

"Leave him alone," said Mrs. Harbock wearily. She waved good-bye before entering the subway.

Mat and Edward did not speak again

till they went through the door of the school building. Edward said, "So long, dummy."

To which Mat replied, "Done it all."

No sooner did he set foot outside his school that afternoon than Mat became one person again and all of that person was excited. He was so excited that he started to run home.

"Hey, what's with you," Edward Harbock's wheezy voice followed him down the street. "Where are you going to anyway? I can hardly keep up." It was a strange thing about Edward. All day in school, he kept as far away from Mat as he could. But no sooner were they out on the street, than Edward was running after Mat to talk to him.

"I have to go home," said Mat, "fast."

"Why, what's up?" Edward panted.

"Oh, nothing." Mat slowed down so that he and Edward walked the rest of the way home together without saying a word until Edward got out of the elevator at his floor and mumbled "Good-bye."

As soon as his mother opened the door Mat flew past her to his room.

"Don't I get a hello?" Mrs. Pit called after him.

"Hello," said Mat.

"There's juice and cookies on the kitchen table," said Mrs. Pit through the door of Mat's room. "Mat," Mrs. Pit's voice rose, "I said, there's juice and cookies and what are you doing in there?"

"Homework," said Mat.

"Really?" said Mrs. Pit with pleasure. "How nice."

Mat sat peering into the vent hole listening to his mother's footsteps outside the door. He wished she would get busy anywhere but in the kitchen so that he could collect some lettuce leaves and a cup of water. As he gazed into the hole he noticed a slight movement and presently

Jester appeared, leaning his paws over the vent's rim.

"Oh, dear boy, we've been waiting for you on tenterhooks. An emergency has arisen." Jester was so out of breath that his thin voice came in gasps. "Remember, remember the rabbit I told you about who's been trying to squeeze in? Well, the most awful thing has happened." Jester trembled all over at the thought. "He's stuck, stuck like a cork in a bottle, been like that all day and suffering, oh, suffer-

ing terribly. He wanted so desperately to join us, you see. He simply detests his life. He lives with a boy who is so unhappy that poor Harry, that's the rabbit's name, can't bear to watch the child another moment. This morning he impulsively tried to ram himself through the vent in a do-or-die effort. Well, it wasn't do and it wasn't die, it was just plain stuck. His head is in, his bottom is out. The boy he lives with just came home from school and you should hear the howl he's putting up. We're all frantic. The sight of that poor stuck creature would make a woodchuck weep."

Jester took a deep breath. "You've got to work it from the other end, Mat."

FOUR

"WHAT'S the apartment?" said Mat.

"South East Wing 14C. Get over there right away."

"What will I tell them?" said Mat, panicking. "I don't know them."

"You'll think of a pretext, I know it," said Jester. "You're so clever."

"I'm not clever," said Mat, but he said it to Jester's retreating tail, for the mouse was gone.

"Where are you going?" said Mrs. Pit, as Mat raced to the front door.

"Have to visit somebody," said Mat.

"A friend?" said Mrs. Pit. "A new friend?"

"Yes," said Mat.

"Oh, how nice," said Mrs. Pit to the closing door.

Out in the hall Mat thought of waiting for the elevator but changed his mind and raced down the two flights of stairs. It wasn't till he'd rung the bell of 14C that he decided he'd ask for a cup of sugar for his mother. He remembered seeing a neighbor doing that on a TV show. The sugar idea went right out of his mind when the door was opened by none other than Edward Harbock. Mat was so surprised he forgot for a moment the reason he had come. Edward was a mess. His eyes were red and dripping tears, his nose was also red and dripping. The sight of Mat startled Edward out of a great shuddering sob.

"What are you doing here?" said Mat.

"I live here," said Edward trying to

pull himself together. He rubbed his eyes. "I'm having an allergy attack," he said.

"Looks like you're crying," said Mat, realizing that Edward was the boy Harry lived with who was so unhappy.

"I can't see you now," said Edward.

"You've got to," said Mat. "You can help me with the math." He pushed past Edward and sped through Edward's foyer and Edward's living room where Mrs. Harbock was talking on the telephone, and into Edward's bedroom where his books were scattered on his bed and his rabbit's cage stood empty.

"Where's your rabbit?" said Mat.

"I don't know," Edward sputtered. "He's gone." Then his sobbing resumed at full blast. Mat got down on all fours and pretended to look under the bed. Then he slowly circled the room on his knees till he reached the radiator cover which he squinted behind. There were two hind legs and a soft white tail trembling in the darkness. "Look," said Mat.

Edward knelt beside Mat and clapped his hands. "Harry," he cried. Then worriedly he whispered, "What do we do?"

Mat gently circled Harry's warm quivering rabbit hind parts with his hands and began to pull. Edward pushed his hand into his mouth to stop a gasp. With a swift movement Harry suddenly popped out. He landed with his front paws sprawled on the floor and his fur all mussed. Edward grabbed him in his arms and smoothed him lovingly.

"My mom says Harry makes me allergic," said Edward, "but I don't care. I wonder why he tried to get in that hole. Boy is he dumb." He kissed the top of Harry's head and thought of something. "I'm sorry I called you dumb this morning, Mat. You're not dumb. You were smart to find Harry. Was it really magic?"

"No," said Mat. "It wasn't magic."

"But how did you know?"

Mat shrugged. He liked to think he had magic but couldn't claim to it when it wasn't true. Especially with Harry listening. Mat looked at Harry. He was miserable. His pink eyes drooped, looking irritated and weepy. "He looks like he has an allergy too," said Mat.

"Maybe he does," said Edward, "only it would have to be to me." He smiled sadly. "My mother says he's making my allergy worse. She wants me to get rid of him."

Suddenly there was a rustling sound coming from under the radiator. Harry turned his head sharply and tried to leap out of Edward's arms but was caught in time. Mat got down on his knees first and saw Jester looking frantic.

"Tragedy has struck, go home immediately," Jester whispered before he ducked back into the hole. He was out of sight by the time Edward got his plump body on the floor.

"I've got to go," said Mat.

"But you just came," said Edward. "Please stay. I'm sorry if I give you a hard time in school. Nobody likes me and I figured since they like you even less, if I talk to you it would be worse for me."

"I've got to go," said Mat, edging toward the door and then breaking into a run. "Maybe I'll see you later."

Mrs. Harbock was still on the telephone as Mat whizzed through the living room. When he got to his own floor he heard shrieks coming through the door of his apartment.

FIVE

MAT pushed the door open to see his mother running around the living room with a broom raised high over her head. For a moment Mat couldn't figure what to make of the scene. His mother was screaming as well as waving the broom. Then Mat saw a small gray mouse dashing under couches and chairs trying to escape the flailing broom.

"Get him, get him!" cried Mrs. Pit to Mat. "He's going for your room." She dashed after the mouse just in time to see him disappear under the radiator in Mat's room. Mrs. Pit fell to her knees and peered under the radiator.

"He's gone," she said. Then she sat

bolt upright. "Wait a minute, I know where he went." She looked under the radiator again. "Merciful heavens, he must have gone in the vent hole. I'll bet that vent is crawling with vermin. CRAWL-ing. Oh, my goodness." The thought of it caused her to bang on the radiator.

"Princess Gardens, my foot," Mrs. Pit yelped. "Rodent Paradise is more like it. When I think of all the money we're paying, too. Oh, Mathew, I've had a shock. I came into your room to prepare your lessons for tonight when out of the corner of my eye I saw this thing streak across the rug. Well you can imagine how I felt when I saw what it was." The recollection made her shudder. She thought for a moment. "I've got to call the landlord," she said. "That's the first thing to do. I've got to tell him what's going on and he will have to do something about it."

Mrs. Pit got to her feet and marched to the telephone in the kitchen. Mat heard her dial, then he heard her ask for the landlord and then he heard her tell about the mouse. Then Mat didn't hear anything until he heard his mother's angry voice say, "Are you telling me that I'm crazy, Mr. Princess or whoever you are? I see I shall get no cooperation from you. I am forced to call my own exterminator and you, sir, shall receive the bill."

Mat heard Mrs. Pit call two exterminators who did not please her and finally one who did. She made an appointment with him for the following morning at ten o'clock.

When the phone call was over, Mrs. Pit had to go down to the market. After the door closed behind her, Mat sat down on the floor near the radiator. In a moment Jester appeared and beside him was Mat's friend Sparky.

Mat forgot the emergency when he saw his old pet. "Sparky!" He picked the gerbil up and held him gently, stroking his silky back. "How are you?" Sparky nuzzled his nose between Mat's fingers but when he lifted his face Mat saw that it was filled with alarm and worry.

"It's bad, isn't it?" Jester said. "It's very bad."

"An exterminator's coming tomorrow morning at ten," Mat said.

"Merciful Muenster," Jester cried, "so little time. We're done for, Mat, done for. The entire community will be wiped out. Oh, that foolish greedy Tobias. I knew he would bring us all to a bad end. No common sense. He has no common sense, and where is a mouse without common sense? I'd have expected this from a guinea pig perhaps, but oh, the shame of it, all being the fault of a mouse." Jester hung his head miserably. "He got mixed up, you see. All these apartments are so alike. He thought he was in 15C where the lady is out all day and leaves lots of crumbs lying around. We were all so upset about Harry that Tobias simply got confused and went to 16C. Now we're done for. It was too good to last."

Jester began to weep and so did Sparky. Small tears rolled over their whiskers and onto the floor.

"But Sparky can come back and live here," said Mat.

Sparky shook his small head violently.

"He would never do that," said Jester. "Much as he likes you, Mat, he'd never leave us at a time like this."

"Then I'll have to save all of you," Mat said without realizing he'd said it.

Jester and Sparky looked up at him together. A tear hung on Sparky's whisker before it dropped. "How?" said Jester.

"Never mind, I will," Mat cried.

"All of us?" said Jester. "You remember, there's a large community."

"All of you," Mat cried again.

"Not that we aren't grateful for the sentiment and all that," Jester said. "But, dear boy, how on earth can you do it? There's not much time and your mother is determined."

"I'll do it," said Mat.

"It isn't just a question of getting out," said Jester. "Remember it's also a question of where do we go when we get out."

"I'll think of something," said Mat.

"Then we'll leave you to think," said Jester. "We must go and help make preparations for leaving."

"Be here tonight at eleven thirty," Mat said. "All of you."

"Very well," Jester whispered. "We have no choice." With a flick of their tails the two small beasts were gone. Mat sat alone on the floor. His head was fairly bursting with all the thinking it had to do.

SIX

MRS. Pit told Mr. Pit about the afternoon's events at dinnertime. Mat could hardly eat a thing.

"Why do you look so grim, young man?" said Mr. Pit over the steaming soup. "Tomorrow's Saturday. Isn't that something to rejoice about? Why when I was your age, on a hot night like this, I'd take my pup tent out to the back yard and set it up and lie down in it and sometimes sleep right there under the stars. Nobody'd ever bother me, it was my own private place." Mr. Pit's eyes grew misty with recollection. He was very fond of recalling things out of his own boyhood and could never understand why the same things weren't happening to Mat that had happened to him.

"This is the city, dear," said Mrs. Pit. "Mat's got no back yard. Of course he does have a tent which you bought for him two years ago and which has never been used."

"That's right, he does have a tent," said Mr. Pit who had bought Mat the small green canvas tent at Macy's and had never even unrolled it.

"And I have got a terrace even if there's no back yard," said Mat, who was beginning to have an idea that was exploding in his head. "Hey, Mom, could I put my tent up on the terrace tonight and sleep under the stars like Dad used to do?"

"I don't know," Mrs. Pit started to say.

"Say, that's a terrific idea," said Mr. Pit. "See, Irma, I told you I didn't throw out money on that thing. He's going to use it."

"But it will take up so much room and the bridge club's coming here to play tomorrow afternoon," said Mrs. Pit. "I thought we'd play on the terrace."

"It will take up only one corner," said Mr. Pit. "There's plenty of room for you ladies."

"Oh, dear, all right," said Mrs. Pit.

"And nobody will bother me?" Mat said. "It will be private just like it was for Dad out in his back yard?"

"It certainly will, Son," said Mr. Pit smiling fondly.

"Just don't mess up the rest of the terrace," said Mrs. Pit.

"I won't," said Mathew who was gulping down the rest of his dinner in great relief and excitement.

Mat and his father set up the tent after supper. Then Mat sat down to do his homework. Finally it was time for bed. He put his sleeping bag into the tent and crawled into it so that his head was half out of the tent. He looked up, not at the stars but at the bottom of the terrace above him. He heard the brakes and the engines of cars down in the street and the voices of people on their terraces and through their open windows. He was happy. He'd have no trouble staying awake. Periodically he heard his parents step onto the terrace to check on him and he closed his eyes and breathed slowly when they did.

"Never thought the kid would stick it out," Mat's father chuckled.

"Let's go to bed, Clifford," said Mrs. Pit. "I've got a big day tomorrow, exterminator in the morning and bridge club in the afternoon."

Soon the apartment was dark. The only sound in it was the refrigerator motor and the electric clock whirring. Mat crept back into his room. He knelt in the dark and peered under the radiator. He took the

small light he had gotten at the circus and flashed it into the vent hole. Out of the darkness dozens of glowing circles stared at him like magic marbles with lights of their own. The eyes followed Mat but there was hardly a sound.

"We're all here," Jester said in a barely audible whisper. "Every one of us, Mat. Now what?"

Mat's knees creaked as he got to his feet. "Follow the light," he said. He beamed the circus light so that it made a circle on the floor.

One by one the rodents scampered out of the vent hole and followed the beam of light out of Mat's room, through the living room, and onto the terrace. Mat held the flap of the tent open so that the tunnel tenants could march easily into their new habitat.

When every creature was inside, Mat laced up the flaps of his tent and climbed into his own bed in his own room. He was very tired and his eyes started to close. He felt a small tickle at his ear.

Jester sat on the pillow. "Thanks, dear boy," he said. "But I can't help wondering, where do we go from here?"

"Don't worry," said Mat. But he *was* worried. He lay awake in the dark trying and trying to think of something, but no plan came to him and soon in spite of himself he was sleeping. It was a sleep full of dreams. Mat dreamed that the creatures were in danger and he was trying to find a magic potion that came in a funny yellow bottle and would make them safe. He dreamt that Sparky was being chased down the vent by the exterminator. He woke up feeling hot and thirsty and knowing that he had no really good plan at all.

SEVEN

"DIDN'T stick it out," Mr. Pit said when Mat came in to the kitchen for breakfast the next morning.

"It was too hard and too noisy," said Mat, "but I'm taking my breakfast into my tent and I would like it to be private, like you said."

"Did you hear that, Irma?" said Mr. Pit. "He's really using it. I knew I wasn't throwing my money away on that thing. Best idea I ever had, getting the boy a pup tent. Maybe he'll ask a friend up to see it."

Mat took his bowl of cereal and milk and a glass of water on a tray. Then he took a half a head of lettuce and a wedge of cheese and a bunch of wilted watercress and hoped his mother wouldn't notice. But she did.

"What on earth are you taking for breakfast?" said Mrs. Pit. "Lettuce and cheese and watercress?"

"I like lettuce and cheese and watercress," said Mat.

"And I like lobster, but I don't eat it for breakfast," said Mrs. Pit.

"But I want to," said Mat.

Mrs. Pit threw up her hands and turned to her husband. "He's eccentric," she said. "Along with everything else he's eccentric." Then she waved him off, "Oh, go eat lettuce for breakfast."

Mat tried not to run with his tray. Inside the tent, looking very still and startled were twenty-seven gerbils, thirty-nine hamsters, sixty mice, and five guinea pigs. They were one on top of the other. All their eyes followed Mat's tray.

He managed to squeeze in. He tore the lettuce into small bits and dropped them among the animals. He broke up the watercress and crumbled the cheese. It made him happy to watch the food so gratefully devoured.

"We're all very thankful to you, Mathew," said Jester, "but I must confess I am too worried to taste a morsel. Surely now that you see us all you realize that this is but temporary shelter. Where will we go from here? We are under a great strain trying not to step on each other. The guinea pigs are large and not too clever. Their natural instinct is to oink all night and we were frantic lest they forget themselves and call attention to our hideout. Their self-control cannot last much longer. The gerbils are frightened out of their wits. The hamsters are picking on them. The mice are bearing up, but even they . . . " Jester's voice trailed off.

"The exterminator will be here at

ten," said Mat, causing a shudder among all the beasts who were listening. "Let me find out what poison he plans to use, how long it will be effective, and when it will be

safe for you to go back to your homes in the tunnel. Then I'll think of the next move."

"We have no choice but to follow your instructions, Mat," said Jester.

"Then eat some cheese," Mat said smiling. "You'll need your strength."

But Jester looked alarmed. "The doorbell is ringing," he said. "Do you suppose it's the . . . it's HIM."

EIGHT

IT wasn't the exterminator. It was Edward Harbock at the door.

"It's Edward Harbock from 14C," Mrs. Pit said. "What a nice surprise. Look who's here to see you, Mat."

Edward Harbock looked very unhappily around him till he saw Mat coming in from the terrace. "I've got to talk to you," he said. They went into Mat's room and Edward closed the door. "Harry won't eat anything. He keeps squeaking and trying to get back into the vent hole. I don't understand what's bothering him."

"What do you want me to do?" said

Mat, hoping to himself that Harry hadn't gotten wind of the trouble in the tunnel and wished to join the community in the pup tent.

"I thought maybe you had some kind of special magic for finding him and maybe you could use it for helping him now," Edward said. "He'll die if he keeps starving himself."

Mat looked at Edward's miserable fat face with its fogged-up glasses and large chipped front tooth and made a very big and perhaps dangerous decision. "Come with me, Edward," he said. "I have something to show you."

Edward looked bewildered as Mat led him out to the terrace, but when Mat pulled back the flaps of the pup tent to reveal its packed inside, Edward began to howl. Mat clamped a hand over Edward's mouth.

"Keep quiet," he said. "Nobody's to know but us two. I'm telling you because I need your help. First of all Harry was trying to join them in the vent system where they all usually live. Yesterday my mom found out about them and she's called an exterminator to come at ten o'clock this morning. They're here for temporary shelter but still we need an escape route in case something unexpected should happen. I just thought of it, Edward. You've got to help."

Edward was throbbing with excitement. His red face was beaming even before Mat asked for his help.

"Good," said Mat, "we have to work fast. We've got to make a tunnel from here to your terrace in case evacuation is called for."

"We need a pipe," said Edward.

"And we need it quick," said Mat.

"Any ideas?" said Edward.

"No," said Mat.

"Oh, boy," said Edward. "Toilet-paper rollers, paper-towel rollers."

"Enough to go down two floors? Impossible. We need something else, quick."

"We can do it," Edward panted. "My mom's got rug rollers. They're hollow. Some are bamboo, but some are cardboard and they're wide. We'll use them and whatever else we've got around."

"What are you two boys doing out there?" said Mr. Pit.

"We're planning a message chute from your terrace to mine," said Edward, thinking so fast that Mat was filled with admiration.

"A message chute, hey, that's a smart idea," Mr. Pit was impressed. "See, Irma, city kids can so have fun. Anything I can do to help out?"

"We need rollers from toilet paper and toweling," said Mat.

"Of course I can't send written messages up the tube, but it can carry my voice and work like a telephone," said Edward.

"Say, that's a cute idea," said Mr. Pit. "Let's see what we've got."

As it turned out what the Pits had was very little. Two toilet-paper rollers and one paper-towel roller. When fastened together with tape these rollers came to not more than two feet. Edward and Mat went down to the Harbocks' to try out the rug rollers. Fortunately, Mrs. Harbock's apartment was full of rugs and their rollers.

The boys spread out everything they had collected on the living room floor in Mat's apartment. They started taping the tubes and rollers together with heavy-duty tape. They put masking tape over the heavy-duty tape and wound reinforced package tape over that. They ran a wire lengthwise down the pipe to prevent it from buckling. Then they carried the pipe carefully out to the terrace. Mat lowered it slowly over the side. It only reached down one floor.

"What's going on?" Miss Zipser, the lady in 15C, called up.

The boys told her.

"Oh, that's nice," she said. "I'll give you another rug roller if you'll let me in on the secret messages." Miss Zipser was a very pleasant lady who made such a racket practicing her bongo drums that she was

not going to complain about a paper pipe-
line passing her terrace. Her rug roller
plus two more paper-towel rollers made
the escape tunnel exactly the right size.

The boys assembled the pipes with
tape and wire and Miss Zipser let them
attach it onto her terrace railing. When it
was secured twice over onto Edward's
railing and Mat's railing, they made a little
curved chute onto the terrace so that the
animals would not be in danger of falling
off.

Mathew felt better than he had all
morning. At least total disaster could be
avoided, he thought, although he certainly
hoped there would be no need to use the
escape route. His thoughts were interrupted by the ringing of the doorbell.

NINE

STANDING at the door was Mr. Bang of Bing Bing and Bang Exterminators Incorporated. Mr. Bang was short and round, and wore very thick glasses. He had a merry mad smile on his face and a large satchel under his arm.

"Mr. Bing?" said Mrs. Pit.

"No, I'm Bang," said Mr. Bang. "I changed my name. Bing Bing and Bing sounded boring. Anyway I'm not like my brothers. They do the bookwork. I do the business. The real business. Now what's the trouble? I hear it's big trouble."

"That's the truth," said Mrs. Pit. "*Vermin.*"

"You don't say," said Mr. Bang, sucking in his breath, his entire face lighting up with excitement. "Now isn't that something. Where are the little buggers hiding out?"

"You won't believe this," said Mrs. Pit.

"Go on, shoot," said Mr. Bang, looking madder and merrier than ever.

"Follow me," said Mrs. Pit.

They walked past Mat and Edward who stood silently at the door of Mat's room and marched right up to the radiator. "Under this clean and modern radiator there is a vent hole," said Mrs. Pit.

Mr. Bang got down on his knees. "So that's it," he said. "A rodent retreat."

"Exactly," Mrs. Pit nodded.

Mr. Bang stood up slowly. His face was as red as a radish and his glasses twinkled crazily. "I have a marvelous mix-

ture that I've never used before," he whispered. "I invented it myself. I've been
waiting for the right time, the right place,
and the right people. It will obliterate
them."

"Now that's the problem," said Mrs.
Pit uncomfortably. "Surely I want them
gone, but if they are killed in there the
unnnnn."

"Dead bodies," Mr. Bang provided.

"Dead bodies would begin to unnnn."

"Smell," Mr. Bang finished gleefully.

"Yes, that's right," said Mrs. Pit.

"And that, dear lady, is what POOF
is all about."

"Poof?" said Mrs. Pit.

"*Poof*," said Mr. Bang with a snap of
the fingers. "Poof, gone, out, finished, and
diminished." Mr. Bang bent down to undo
the straps of his satchel. Slowly he opened
it in such a way that Edward and Mat and
Mr. and Mrs. Pit couldn't see what was
inside it. "My brothers have tormented me

over the years, ever since I told them my idea for *Poof*. They teased me all the while I worked in my laboratory. They told me I was mad. They told me it couldn't be done, but HA HA HA." Mr. Bang bellowed the laugh in such a surprising way that Mr. and Mrs. Pit and the boys took a step backward. "I did it. I did it."

He plucked a small yellow bottle out of his satchel and held it up. It seemed to glow a firefly kind of pale glow. "There it is, my *Poof*." Mr. Bang beamed lovingly at the bottle. "You lucky Pits will be the first to have the benefit of it."

Mrs. Pit looked very unhappy. "I don't know," she said. "I don't want to be an experiment."

"Not you, dear lady," said Mr. Bang. "You will be fine, but our fine furry friends will be . . . Poof."

"What does *Poof* do?" said Mr. Pit matter-of-factly.

"It shrinks them down," said Mr.
Bang with a delighted snort.

"Down down down, smaller smaller
smaller, till they're gone. Completely

gone. No fuss, no smell, no dead bodies, no mess, in short everything clean and tidy."

"How nice," said Mrs. Pit in spite of herself, for she was beginning to think Mr. Bang was very peculiar indeed. "How do you get it to them?"

"Simply pour three drops of *Poof* on a piece of cheese and put it in the trouble spot. Then the vapors will permeate the area even if no cheese is nibbled and within three hours every little beast will be . . ."

"Poof," said the Pits, Mat, and Edward all together.

"Precisely," said Mr. Bang. "Now for the cheese."

"Irma, the cheese," said Mr. Pit.

"Mat, the cheese," said Mrs. Pit.

Mat got a wedge of cheese.

"Perfect," said Mr. Bang. They all watched as he opened the bottle of *Poof* and let three glowing drops of yellowy fluid drip onto the cheese. Then they watched as he placed the wedge of the cheese on the rim of the vent. As he levered himself onto his feet everyone sighed.

Mr. Bang put the *Poof* back in his satchel and wiped his hands on a plaid handkerchief. "That will be twenty-seven dollars and eighty cents," he said. "Call me if you have any further problems, though I can't believe you ever will. *Poof* is perfect. If it doesn't work, of course I always have my bomb——"

"Bomb!" said Mrs. Pit, horrified.

"It's the final answer," said Mr. Bang. "It kills completely. Just drop it in, pull the pin, and poison gas. The buggers haven't got a chance."

Mr. Pit gave him a check and Mr. Bang left, waving it above his head as he waited for the elevator.

"He was a little strange, wasn't he?" said Mrs. Pit, when they were alone again.

"He must be a genius," said Mr. Pit. "Who ever heard of a thing like *Poof?*"

"We have, Clifford," said Mrs. Pit worriedly, "and I hope we don't regret it."

Mathew Pit and Edward Harbock, who had been silent through all these doings, hoped so, too. But ever since he had seen the gleamy glowing bottle of *Poof*, Mat had heard a strange ringing in his ears, felt a tingling in his back hairs and a rodent sense of trouble in his human boy head. When the doorbell began to jangle and the bridge club players to arrive he nearly jumped with agitation.

TEN

THE ladies were all seated at Mrs. Pit's card table out on the corner of the terrace just beside the umbrella tree. Behind the umbrella tree, next to the door to the living room, was Mat Pit's pup tent chock-full of what Mrs. Pit referred to as vermin. At the door, their eyes big and their faces pale, were Mat and Edward.

"Tonight, when the lights are out, I'll take the cheese and flush it down the toilet," Mat was saying. "Then I'll lead the creatures back."

"But what if the vapors of *Poof* are still dangerous?" said Edward. "Maybe you ought to take it out earlier and risk your mother's not checking to see if it's still there."

"I'll try it," said Mat. "I don't know how much longer they can hold out. The air is pretty stuffy in there."

"Mathew dear," Mrs. Pit called. "Could you and your friend bring in the tray of lemonade and cookies now. We're ever so thirsty."

Reluctantly Mat and Edward left their position by the door and shuffled into the kitchen where a tray of glasses and cookies was ready on the counter. Mat took a pitcher of iced lemonade out of the refrigerator and put it on the tray. He hoisted the tray, and walked carefully, trying not to upset the tinkling glasses or spill the lemonade. Though the tray was large and cumbersome Mat was doing very well—until he reached the door to the terrace. He didn't remember to step down, and he toppled.

Edward grabbed the tray just as Mat fell, so nothing was broken, but poor Mat fell right down on the pup tent which collapsed beneath him. The ladies' bridge club screamed to see him fall, but that was nothing to what they did when they saw twenty-seven gerbils, thirty-nine hamsters, sixty mice, and five guinea pigs scamper out from under the green canvas.

Pandemonium reigned. Mrs. Miller fainted straight off. Mrs. Armbruster had a seizure. Mrs. Lerner hopped up and down saying hup hup hup, and Mrs. Pit stood up on the table and said aaaghrsgh, yechhhh, and other sounds that are hard to write down in letters. Mr. Pit ran in from the bedroom and stood still as a statue at the door. In the middle of the confusion Mat caught Jester's eye. "The escape tunnel!" he yelled.

Jester ran to the cardboard pipe Mat pointed at and dove into it. The other members of the community followed him

and in a matter of three minutes the stream of scampering animals was gone. Their evacuation was so speedy and organized that the four women and Mr. Pit stood in hushed disbelief wondering if they had all shared a dream and not witnessed an actual event at all.

Mrs. Pit came down off the table. "Did anybody see what I saw?" she asked timidly.

Mrs. Miller opened her eyes, fluttering the lids. "What happened?" she said. "Where did they all go?"

"Yes," said Mrs. Armbruster. "Where did they all go?" Then for the first time everyone turned and looked at Mat and Edward.

"Am I crazy or did you say something to them, Mathew Pit?" said Mrs. Pit.

"Who me?" said Mat.

Luckily, then Mrs. Pit thought of something. "Merciful heavens, Edward Harbock, your poor dear mother. They'll be all over her terrace. Girls, we've got to go tell Mrs. Harbock."

The bridge club got up from their seats somewhat shakily and marched as a group down to apartment 14C. Edward and Mat followed. Mrs. Harbock was slow in coming to the door for she had been practicing her violin.

"What can I do for you, ladies?" she said.

"Dear Dorothea," said Mrs. Pit, "I don't know how to begin. We were just having some lemonade when . . . "

"Your terrace is swarming with vermin," Mrs. Armbruster screeched. "Swarming."

"I beg your pardon," said Mrs. Harbock, looking very icy. "My terrace is clean as a whistle."

"This isn't meant to insult you, Dorothea," said Mrs. Pit. "But really it's true."

"Of course it insults me," said Mrs.

Harbock. "You're implying that my house is sloppy."

"No no no no not that," Mrs. Pit protested. "The creatures descended from my own terrace to yours through the children's message tube. Please—may we investigate?"

Grudgingly Mrs. Harbock let the ladies in, but their conversation at the door had given the community just enough time to hide in the planters full of bushes on the Harbocks' terrace. By the time the ladies reached the terrace, not a rodent was in sight.

"There," said Mrs. Harbock. "If this is some kind of joke I'm afraid I fail to get the humor of it."

"Do you mind if I pull out one of those to have a look?" said Mrs. Pit, pointing to one of the planters.

"Yes, I do mind," said Mrs. Harbock. "I mind very much. You've come in here

and interrupted my practice time. You tell
me my terrace is crawling with rats and
now you want to start dismantling it for
me. No, thank you. I suggest that if you

see swarms of vermin on my terrace, there may have been something a little stronger in your lemonade than lemons."

Mrs. Pit looked very angry. "Are you suggesting that we've been drinking?" she yelped.

"Either that or you're nuts," said Mrs. Harbock coolly.

"Oh," said Mrs. Miller. "This is most insulting." She turned and stomped out. The other ladies followed her, their cheeks bright red with anger.

Mrs. Harbock went back to her violin, while Mat and Edward went out to the terrace and collapsed on the floor. It was then that Mat saw many small eyes twinkling at him through the bushes.

ELEVEN

"EVERY one of you will have to stay here until Mat gives us the all clear," said Edward. "He'll remove the *Poof* as soon as he can, and as soon as it's safe for you, you will return to your homes."

"How will you know if it's safe?" said Jester.

"Mr. Bang said it would do the job in three hours, so let's give it more time than that just to be sure," said Mat. "I'll try to remove the *Poof* this afternoon, but I don't think you should go back to your homes until midnight."

"Okay," Jester said. "At least I hope it's okay."

To be honest, Mat and Edward had their doubts about how okay it would be. Things hadn't been going too smoothly for them that morning. In spite of their troubles they felt a certain pleasure and excitement in their lives that was new. The pleasure of working together in secrecy and danger to try to save the lives of an entire community of creatures made them happy. It also made them hungry.

They went to the kitchen and ate six baloney sandwiches between them. Then they went up to 16C, and polished off all the cookies the bridge club had been too upset to eat.

The bridge club ladies were too upset to play bridge. They sat out on the terrace discussing the events of the morning. Mrs. Lerner said, "Irma, I'd call Mr. Bang back here immediately. Tell him the problem's greater than you realized."

"Call the landlord," said Mrs. Armbruster, "it's his responsibility. Vermin in a building are the landlord's responsibility."

"I called him once and he implied that I was seeing things," said Mrs. Pit. "I won't be insulted by him again. Frankly, I don't want to call Mr. Bang just yet. I'd very much like to see Dorothea Harbock eat her words. When that little army of rodents marches out onto her terrace one fine day I say let *her* have the pleasure of calling Mr. Bang and paying twenty-seven dollars and eighty cents for a dose of *Poof*."

"You know, I don't think all those creatures were rats and mice," said Mrs. Lerner. "One of them oinked as it passed my chair."

"My dear, I wouldn't be surprised if one of them mooed," said Mrs. Miller. "This whole thing is too fantastic."

The bridge club sat about sipping lemonade and chatting in this way for much of the afternoon, while Mr. Pit watched a ball game on television. Mat and Edward retired to Mat's room, closed the door, and carefully removed the *Poof*-filled wedge of cheese. Mat took it to the bathroom and flushed it down the toilet.

"They'll be able to go back even sooner than midnight, provided your parents go to bed early," said Mat happily.

"No chance for that," said Edward. "Tonight is Saturday night."

"What does Saturday night have to do with it?" said Mat.

"My mother's string quartet," said Edward. "They play chamber music at our apartment every Saturday night." He paused. "In the living room."

"Life is full of complications," said Mat gloomily. If it wasn't a bridge club it was a string quartet. How much more simple it would be to live in a vent shaft and be a gerbil. Mat and Edward tried to play checkers just to pass the time.

"Maybe we could get them in at six o'clock," said Edward.

"I wouldn't risk it," said Mat. "*Poof* sounds like powerful stuff. We took it out of the vent at three o'clock. We better wait till after dinner at least."

"When the string quartet is still playing up a storm," said Edward.

"I hope it's the only storm we have tonight," said Mat.

TWELVE

HOW he got through supper that night, Mat wasn't sure. He helped clear the table and listened to his mother talk about the "thing" that had happened that day. Finally it was eight o'clock. His parents were so distracted that they forgot to pester him about his schoolwork.

Mat went to his room where he tried to read. He was simply looking at letters, not thinking of them at all, and was so prickly and anxious that he couldn't seem to sit still in one spot. Finally he left his room. He tiptoed past the living room where his parents were watching TV. He let himself out the front door without a creak.

When Mat got to Edward's floor he noticed that the door of the Harbocks' apartment was slightly open. He just walked in. The chairs in the living room were arranged with music stands in front of them. Mrs. Harbock's voice was coming from Edward's bedroom.

Mat saw Edward seated at his desk and Mrs. Harbock standing behind him.

"You've got three more chapters to finish," she said.

"But I'm already five chapters ahead of everybody else," Edward complained, dabbing at his nose.

"I don't care about everybody else," said Mrs. Harbock. "I want you to be best."

Harry gazed gloomily out of his cage and Edward sneezed loudly.

"Oh, that rabbit's got to go," said

Mrs. Harbock. "It's perfectly ridiculous keeping him. Your allergy is getting worse and worse."

"I want to keep Harry," said Edward.

"If only you could think of a way to keep Harry, but not his fur all over your room," said Mrs. Harbock.

"What if I can't think of a way?" said Edward.

"Then he's got to go. By next Monday. Now back to your books, sir. We don't want your brains to get rusty, or you won't be smartest."

"I don't want to be smartest," Edward wailed.

"Oh, yes, you do," said Mrs. Harbock. "Now finish that page."

As Edward bent his head over the workbook, Mat realized why Harry couldn't stand to live at 14C. Mrs. Harbock was as fierce as Mrs. Pit, but Edward was smart and Mat was stupid. Mat thought, it doesn't matter if you're smart or dumb. Edward was getting it just as hard as he was.

Mat was surprised out of his thoughts when the doorbell rang.

"That would be the quartet," said Mrs. Harbock looking up. "Why, Mat Pit," she said seeing him for the first time, "what are you doing here? I didn't even hear you come in." She turned back to Edward. "Now, Edward, I want you to finish up that work before you start visiting with Mat."

Edward didn't say anything. The boys watched Mrs. Harbock sweep out of the room. Soon after that the lovely music of the quartet filled the apartment.

Edward put down his pen, pushed his glasses up on his nose, and sighed deeply. "Boy, am I glad to see you, old buddy. This business makes me very nervous."

"How have they been?" said Mat.

"Okay, I guess. I've had things to do

in here for a while so I haven't been able to get out to them. As soon as the quartet leaves and my folks are asleep, I'll tell them the coast is clear."

"Good," said Mat. "Let's check on the escape route." He walked to the door of Edward's room. "We want to be sure there's no furniture blocking their path. They'll have to move quickly."

Edward opened the door. The boys looked into the living room and what they saw there caused them both to freeze.

THIRTEEN

MRS. Harbock's string quartet, completely lost in the music they were playing, did not notice that through the open door onto the terrace, there came not only a gentle and fragrant spring breeze, but three gray mice as well. The mice, nodding their heads in ecstatic appreciation of the music, were followed by two guinea pigs and a hamster. The creatures moved slowly into the living room and arranged themselves around the edge of the rug, swaying to the music's rhythm.

The lady who played the cello suddenly saw what the others did not. Mat and Edward saw her see and both of them felt their hearts fall into their shoes. Mrs. Pingot, for that was the cellist's name, called out, "Dorothea, what a charming scene," she pointed with her bow at the rodents.

The music stopped. All eyes turned. All eyes opened wide in disbelief. "Why, they're adorable," said Mrs. Pingot. "Lapping up the sounds like little concert-

goers. Where ever did you find them?"

"Oh, my goodness," said Mrs. Harbock, casting a worried glance out to the terrace, "I think I know."

"I'll bet this is one of Edward's wonderful ideas, training rodents in music," said Mr. Pingot, who held a viola. "The boy's a genius."

"Edward," Mrs. Harbock called proudly. "Come here, darling."

Edward bounded through the door. "Mr. Pingot wonders if you trained the mice in music appreciation."

"Not really," said Edward with his eyes down and his ears crimson.

"Well, it certainly is nice to play for an audience," Mr. Harbock exclaimed, tucking his violin under his chin. The quartet resumed and the rest of the community of creatures trailed through the door and into the living room.

"What a cultured household you have, Dorothea," whispered Mrs. Pingot.

"Even the mice are musical."

As the music continued, Mat beckoned to Jester to follow him into Edward's bedroom.

"I think it's time you returned to your homes," said Mat. "Now, while no one is watching. Even if it means missing the rest of the concert. I know it's before schedule, but the *Poof* should be gone by now."

"I agree," said Jester. "People, as I have said before, are not to be trusted. They think we're adorable now, because we're enjoying the music and they never knew we could. But when it's all over we'll be revolting vermin again. They'll go running to that Mr. Bang. I'll summon the community right now."

Jester moved quickly among his friends. One by one they stole from the living room into Edward's room, under the radiator, and into the vent hole. Only Jester remained to see everyone safely out of sight. When the last little mouse dawdled, Jester reprimanded him. "You started this escapade, Tobias Mouse. Now you're almost the last to see the end of it. This will teach you a lesson, never forsake your common sense again." The mouse leaped into the vent.

Through all this, Harry the rabbit sat with his face pressed to the wires of his cage, squeaking miserably. Jester looked over at him. "This is very hard on him, you know," he said. "I don't know what to tell him that would cheer him up. It's all a question of size, poor Harry."

Edward looked over at his wretched pet. "He'll be gone by Monday if I can't think of a way to stop being allergic to his fur in my room."

Jester turned to Mat and Edward. "One problem after another," he sighed. "I hope at least this ugly business is over with." But as he spoke the doorbell was ringing and a new commotion had started in the living room.

FOURTEEN

MAT and Edward ran to the door of the living room. They saw that Mr. and Mrs. Pit had arrived. Mrs. Pit was saying, "I am so sorry to intrude on your music, Dorothea, but there is something I must discuss with you." Mrs. Pit suddenly saw Mat standing there. "Why, Mat, when did you get down here?" She stared at her son in amazement.

"I must apologize to you, Irma, before you say another word," said Mrs. Harbock. "The little creatures you mentioned this afternoon are indeed here."

"Precisely," said Mrs. Pit. "I've just

calmed down enough to put together what happened. They were not affected by the exterminator's *Poof*. That is clear to me now. They were not even in the vent when he used the stuff. We need to take some new action."

"But they love music," said Mrs. Pingot, waving her bow aloft. "They stood right in that corner and listened to us play, the little dears."

"When they aren't listening to music, however, they are destroying and dirtying," said Mrs. Pit. "I think they're horrid. They don't belong in a building. Tomorrow morning I am calling Mr. Bang back. I will ask him to use his nerve gas bomb for rodents. It's the only answer. And if the landlord won't pay for it, I do hope that other tenants will contribute to its cost."

Mrs. Harbock rubbed her brow thoughtfully, and looked over at Mr. Harbock. "I don't know," she said. "I really don't know. They were awfully sweet just now."

"Adorable," said Mrs. Pingot.

"But they do of course dirty and destroy and chew things up," said Mrs. Harbock.

"Yes, and the thought of them simply

roaming freely through the vent doesn't give me pleasure," said Mr. Harbock. "I think we should have them bombed out, Mrs. Pit. I'll contribute to the cost."

Mat and Edward closed the door of the bedroom and sat on the floor. Their spirits were lower than that.

"What now?" said Edward. "I think the jig's up."

"It can't be," said Mat. "We've got to think of something. We're responsible for them. They trust us. Let's think, we've got to think." Mat squeezed his head between both his hands as if to force an idea out of it. "Wait a minute, wait a minute," he whispered. "The vent, where does it go?"

"From apartment to apartment," said Edward.

"Up and down, up and down. Up to the roof and down to the basement."

Edward began to get excited. "Up to the roof. They could go to the roof."

Mat shook his head. "It can be cold

and wet and windy up there," he said.

"Down to the basement."

"That's warm and protected," said Mat. "But we don't know which part of the basement this vent ends up in."

"Let's find out," said Edward. The gloom of a few minutes before had lifted. "Get Jester up here."

Mat kneeled by the vent and called softly. In a second Jester appeared.

"I know," said the mouse gravely. "I heard your mother. It's even worse than before."

"Where does the vent end up? In which part of the basement?" said Mat.

"Why I have no idea," said Jester and then he added a bit snobbishly, "We're all apartment pets you know. We've never been down there."

"Go down now, as far as you can," said Mat. "Then come right back here and tell us where you come out."

Jester was off without a word.

FIFTEEN

"IT'S a big room with white metal shapes like boxes in it and they have shiny knobs on them and dials and everything smells of soap."

"The laundry room. It's the laundry room," Edward cried. "That's it. Tomorrow when Bang comes, all of you go down to the laundry room. We'll hide you in the big machines."

"Unless someone wants to use them," said Mat. "In which case . . . "

"In which case we fry or drown," Jester finished his sentence with a shudder.

"Oh," said Edward. "I hadn't thought of that."

"Well, think of it," said Mat. "People go in and out of that room all day long to use the machines."

Edward was suddenly gloomy again. Jester sniffed unhappily.

"How can we keep everybody out of the laundry room while Bang explodes his bomb?" Mat squeezed his head again.

"Put an OUT OF ORDER sign on the door," said Edward.

"They'd just call a repair man in no time," said Mat. "People have to do their laundry."

"Let's do it for them," Edward bellowed, whacking his hands on his knees with the surprise of what he thought was a terrific idea.

"They'd be suspicious," said Mat.

"Then we'll charge. We'll charge five cents a load and they don't have to hang around waiting for the clothes to get done.

We'll run it through the machines, wash and dry and even fold. They'll leave us the coins plus five cents."

"It's a good idea," said Mat.

"Thank you," Edward said. "I owed you a good idea."

SIXTEEN

NEITHER Mat nor Edward got much sleep that night. They met down in the laundry room soon after breakfast. Mrs. Pit had become kinder to Mat since he started to be friendly with Edward and go around on his own. She smiled at him a lot and didn't pester him at breakfast about his plans and his homework. Mat simply told her he had a date with Edward Harbock and she simply smiled and said, "Run along then, dear. Have a nice time."

As soon as he saw him Mat noticed that Edward was carrying something in a towel under his arm. Mat was about to ask what it was when he saw Harry's face poke out. The rabbit actually looked cheerful in his red-eyed droopy way. "I thought he could join them down here at least for a while," said Edward. "Anyway he stopped squeaking when I told him."

Mat stroked the rabbit's soft ears.

"Bang is coming at nine thirty," Mat told Edward. He consulted his watch. "That's one hour from now."

"What do we do?" Edward yawned. He wasn't used to missing a night's sleep.

"We get them all down here and into one of the machines and then we wait for customers," said Mat.

"Everybody will think we're doing it to make money," said Edward.

"I hope that's what they think," said Mat. "Otherwise they may want to barge in and do their own wash."

It wasn't long before a small round woman, in slippers and curlers and a house dress, pushed a shopping cart filled with laundry up to the door.

"We'd be happy to do your laundry for you, ma'am," said Edward.

"Only five cents for our services and you can relax in your apartment."

"We'll deliver when it's done for no extra charge," Edward chimed in with the new idea. "Just tell us your number and give us your quarters."

The woman's sleepy face smiled delightedly. "Oh, you sweet kids," she piped. "A nickel's too cheap. I'd be happy to pay a dime. I'm going back to sleep. What a terrific Sunday morning this turned out to be." She thrust the change into Edward's hand. "I'm Mrs. Lipsit in 10A," she called as she headed back to the elevator.

Edward sighed with relief.

No sooner had Mrs. Lipsit left, than the animals started to arrive at the end of the vent hole. They were all curious about the laundry room.

"Don't dawdle," Jester pleaded. "Get us into the machine."

While Edward loaded Mrs. Lipsit's clothes into the washer, Mat loaded the animals into one of the two large dryers.

When they were all in, Mat partially closed the door. Edward dropped coins into the washer, shook one cup of soap over the clothes and flicked the dial.

As the machine started, the boys allowed themselves a hoot of laughter. So far, so good, but could it last? Jester's worried little face peering at them from behind the dryer's porthole window stopped their laughing completely. They were not out of danger.

The sight of Sally Loomis, aged ten, and her brother Jake, aged eight, dissolved the boys' good cheer. Sally was hefting a large laundry basket, and Jake held a pail with three boxes in it. The Loomises had always avoided Mat. They seemed very intent on what they were doing. They had no spare time for anyone or anything. Now they were intent on doing their laundry. Mat had a sinking feeling that nobody was going to stop them.

Sally eyed Mat and Edward suspiciously. "Is that machine free?" She pointed to the empty washer.

"Yes and no," said Edward.

"What are you talking about?" said Jake.

"We're doing wash for people today at only a nickel extra charge and free delivery. Just leave your laundry with us and enjoy the morning." Edward laughed weakly.

"We do our own wash, thank you very much," Sally said. "I'm not throwing my nickels around today." She pushed past Edward and opened the machine. She dropped the clothes in very carefully and then arranged them. "The soap, Jake," she said.

Jake handed her the soap.

"Borax."

He handed her the borax.

"Cleaning booster."

He handed her the cleaning booster.

Edward and Mat watched her mea-

sure out the proper amounts of soap and borax and booster in a measuring cup. She looked like a scientist. Slowly she sprinkled the soaps in among the clothes, arranging them again to her liking. When she was satisfied, she pulled out the dial and shut the lid.

"Are you going to dry those, too?" Mat croaked.

"Of course," said Sally. Her gaze drifted over to the dryer. "Do you have some objec . . . " She stopped in the middle of the word and her mouth fell open. "Oh, wait a minute," she gasped. "Holy smoke, Jake. Jake, I just saw Boris." She was pointing to the window of the dryer. Jake dropped the pail.

"Where?"

"Look, look," Sally waved excitedly. "I know it was Boris. Boris was just looking at me."

Mat and Edward exchanged a panic-filled glance.

SEVENTEEN

"OPEN the door, Jake," said Sally.

Mat ran to the dryer and stood in front of it shielding the window with his hands. "No, you can't do that," he said.

"My guinea pig is in there. I know it," said Sally. "I just saw him. We've been looking for him for two months."

"He is in there," said Mat. "They're all in there."

"All?" said Sally and Jake together.

"All," said Mat. Then, while the two washers whirred and spun, Mat and Edward told the whole story. Sally and Jake listened in rapt admiration. They laughed at the escape tunnel adventure and gasped over the visit of Mr. Bang.

When the story was done, Sally grew very thoughtful. Her two straight black brows lowered over the top of her glasses. "We've got to find a real solution to this problem," she said. "You've both been heroes, but your luck can't keep holding. You've been running all the time. Sooner or later the escapes won't work. We need a plan—a good plan."

Sally was right, and Mat knew it. He and Edward had school on Monday, not to mention the rest of the week. They couldn't be there constantly to cope with emergencies. The situation was very dangerous. They needed a good and lasting plan.

"Why don't we each take our animals back home again," said Jake, "and sell the babies that have been born."

Mat caught sight of Jester's tragic face

reacting to this idea. "They won't do that," said Mat. "They are very firm about it. They want to live together in their own community. They will never live in separate cages again."

"Like at the zoo," said Sally. "At the zoo the animals are kept in lovely open spaces with lots of room to hide and play."

"Yes," said Mat. "The vent pipe gave them that."

"They can't use the vent anymore," said Sally. "That's obvious, but just a minute. . . . " She lifted her finger in the air as if to hook an idea with it. "What about a zoo?"

"A zoo?" said Mat.

"Not a real one, but a nice private sort of zoo. A zoo for the animals of Princess Gardens Terrace. Listen, my father is great at building things. He can show us how. Why can't we set up something right here in the building with wire and wood and bits of old cages? It can have runs and tunnels and exercise wheels and soft dark places."

"Good idea," said Mat. "We can all care for the animals, feed them and keep the zoo clean."

"Anybody who lives in this building can volunteer to work on it and everyone can come and watch it and enjoy it," Sally added.

Edward suddenly gasped and then smiled till tears sprouted from his eyes. "That's it, that's it," he squeaked. "I could keep Harry, but not his fur all over my room. It's the answer. That's it. It's a miracle. It's really a miracle. I can't believe it. My parents would let me keep him."

At the word parents Mat grew sullen. "We'll have to tell our parents," he said.

"What's wrong with that?" said Sally. "Mine would love to help."

Mat didn't say anything, but he thought of his mother and her calls to Mr.

Bang and talks of vermin and he somehow didn't think she'd love to help, except with a stronger dose of *Poof*.

"Come on," said Edward, "it's nine thirty. We've got to tell your mother the plan before Bang drops his Rodent Bomb."

Mat agreed, though he certainly was worried. The three of them (Jake was left behind to guard the animals) went up to Mat's apartment. When Mrs. Pit opened the door to them, they saw Mr. Bang behind her. He was removing a nasty-looking greenish metal container from his case.

EIGHTEEN

"DON'T do anything," Mat cried out.

"Please wait," said Sally.

Mr. Bang looked up in surprise. Mr. Pit came out of the living room. Mrs. Pit took a step backward.

"The animals you want to destroy are all our lost pets," said Sally.

"Those odious little buggers, *pets?*" said Mr. Bang with a laugh. "That's a howl." And he proceeded to howl in a very odd way.

"But it's true," said Mat in a loud clear voice. "Sparky's there and Sally's guinea pig Boris and Edward's rabbit Harry and a whole bunch of other pets from this building. They all escaped into the vent to live a better life and that's where they lived happily until Mr. Bang tried to *Poof* them."

"Then we saved them. Me and Mat," said Edward.

"Well, I'll be," Mr. Pit exclaimed.

Mrs. Pit was simply staring at Mat. An amazed smile crept over her face. "Mathew," she said. "You did all that with the tent and the pipes? Why that was very very clever of you dear, and ingenious and brave."

Mat stared at his mother. She was proud of him. He couldn't believe it.

"Now we want to put the animals in a zoo of their own," Sally said, "and we need help."

"A zoo?" said Mr. Pit.

Sally described the zoo they wanted.

"That's a fine idea," said Mrs. Pit. "I

like it much better than having them skittering around the vent. What do you think, Mr. Bang?"

Mr. Bang's glasses glittered angrily. "I think I ought to bomb the livin' daylights out of the buggers and save you the trouble of a zoo."

Mat and his friends gasped and so did the Pits.

"I'm afraid we won't need your services," said Mrs. Pit. "You can put the bomb away. I didn't realize we were dealing with pets when I called you in."

"I wasted a morning on a couple a nuts," said Mr. Bang sourly.

"Pay the man for his precious time, Clifford," said Mrs. Pit with a wave of her hand. "And send him on his way."

When Mr. Bang was gone, Mrs. Pit telephoned the landlord to ask his permission.

"You know those vermin I called you about the other day?" she said sweetly.

"The ones in the vent? I've discovered from the children in this building that they are a bunch of long-lost pets. Yes indeed."

There was a great deal of clicking on the line and then a high voice which the children could not make out, even though Mrs. Pit held the phone away from her ear. After a few minutes the voice stopped.

Mrs. Pit cleared her throat and continued. "I can certainly understand your distress, sir. As you know I was very concerned myself when I learned of the animals' tenancy in the vent. In fact I was

going to call my lawyer, withhold my rent, and organize the tenants to take action with the Board of Health." Mrs. Pit laughed. "But thanks to the children, the animals are no longer in the vent." Mrs. Pit paused again and listened to the voice at the other end of the phone. "Where are they?" she said softly. "Why, they're in a dryer down in the laundry room."

There was a sputtering sound coming from the receiver.

"Now, that's what I've called you about," said Mrs. Pit comfortingly. "It is a disgrace. You're absolutely right. And now, I'll tell you what I'll do for you. I will not call my lawyer, withhold my rent, or do anything unpleasant to you, if you let the children build a zoo for their pets in one of the basement rooms of this building."

Mrs. Pit took a deep breath while the sputtering sounds issued explosively from the telephone. She held the telephone away from her ear until the angry voice had run down and then she said sweetly, "The Board of Health would be very upset to learn that you had allowed those animals to wander around through the vent system of your building disregarding the warnings of a tenant. They would be more upset by that than by the presence of a tidy little zoo supervised by children and their parents."

Mrs. Pit listened again, then she said, "I'm sorry if you think that I'm threatening you, but I am very happy that you agree to let the children make a menagerie in the package room."

Mrs. Pit hung up slowly. The children cheered the news and thanked Mrs. Pit. Mr. Pit suggested they start collecting lumber and wire to construct the zoo.

Mat looked at his parents carefully. They were the same people they had always been, but he had never before been so pleased that they were his.

NINETEEN

SALLY called her father to help build the zoo. Edward posted a notice in the lobby advising all families in the building who had lost a gerbil, hamster, mouse, or guinea pig to meet at noon in the laundry room.

While Sally and Mat and Edward went off with Mr. Pit and Mr. Loomis to a lumberyard, Jake continued at his post by the dryer, telling anyone who wanted to use it that it was out of order.

At noon several puzzled children straggled into the laundry room. Mat, Edward, Sally, and the two fathers had arrived with the building materials.

"You talk to them, Mat," said Edward. "You started it all."

Mat had never been able to talk in front of people without losing his voice. "I have an announcement," he said. He had to stop for a moment, because his voice sounded so strong that he didn't recognize it. "Those of you who have lost your pets may have a nice surprise." He opened the dryer door. The room full of children grew silent.

The community of creatures clustered around the open porthole. Their expressions were as fearful as the children's were delighted.

"Just a minute," Mat raised his hands as the children started to swarm around their pets. "These animals have been in hiding because they do not like living alone in cages. They want to stay together as a community. So we have gotten permission to build a zoo for them here in the basement." Mat turned toward Jester and spoke to his worried wise face. "It will have runs and hutches and tunnels and cozy places to sleep and hide. It will be kept tidy by a zoo committee. The animals will not be abused or mistreated in any way."

Jester's expression seemed to change. His eyes glowed warmly. Mat was the only one to hear him murmur, "Thank you, dear boy. I always knew you'd come through."

TWENTY

AND so all that afternoon the children hammered and sawed, working under Mr. Loomis's instructions. By dinnertime the zoo was ready to hold its occupants. Carefully the children carried their animals to the new home, along with exercise wheels, cedar shavings, water dishes, and other equipment from their apartments. Judging by the scampering and preening and whirring around, it appeared the creatures were delighted. The zoo contained tunnels, areas for nesting, nurseries, exercise runs, wheels, and slides. There were watering places and

areas for food. A chart was made up by Sally and Edward listing the feeding times, who was to do the feeding, and how much food was to be given.

Mat and Edward were on their way to the laundry room to get Jester, who wished to be the last to leave the dryer, when a voice rang out behind them: "Young man, come over here." Edward turned slowly.

"Me?" he said.

"You," said the voice which turned out to be that of Mrs. Lipsit. "Where is my laundry?" Mrs. Lipsit was now very wide awake and very angry.

"Oh, my gosh," said Edward, "I forgot."

"You're telling me you forgot," said Mrs. Lipsit. "I left it with you seven hours ago. Some service."

"I'll return your nickel," said Edward. "The clothes are still in the washer."

"In a cold wet bunch?" said Mrs. Lipsit. "You didn't even dry them?"

"No, you see we had our pets in the other dryer and we had to build a zoo for them," said Mat.

Mrs. Lipsit stared at him and a funny look came on her face. "You had your pets in the dryer?" she said slowly. "You poor kid." While she removed her clothes from the washer she kept muttering how hard city life and its pressures could be on children.

Mat opened the dryer door carefully and lifted Jester out. Jester had wanted to be the last so he could make sure that all the other creatures were removed safely. When Mrs. Lipsit saw the tiny mouse cupped in Mat's hand, her eyes grew as round as the frames of her glasses.

After they were out of the laundry room, Mat and Edward laughed till they gasped and tears rolled down their cheeks.

Mat showed Jester the zoo. The mouse looked everything over very carefully and was happy with what he saw.

"I'm very pleased, Mat," said the mouse. "It will be good to live without crises hanging over us." He looked kindly at Mat. "I don't feel sorry for you any more, Mat Pit. You have friends, parents who love you, and . . . " he paused, "you have a quality I rate very high. You have good common sense. We owe you our lives."

Mat stroked the mouse's silken head gently. "I owe you something, too," he said. "I didn't know I had those things."

"And now you won't forget, will you?" said Jester.

Mat lowered him into the zoo careful-ly. "No," he said. "I won't forget."